TABLE OF CONTENTS

Prequel

THE PATH

The samurai warlord Todosi is dead. Now it falls to his brother, a simple monk, to protect his tradition-bound nation from enemies at home and abroad.

Chapters 1 & 2

NEGATION

After the passage of the Nightwall, Kaine and the other abductees find themselves in lockdown within an alien prison. The special abilities of Evinlea and the others remain scrambled, but Kaine has a plan to escape.

Chapters 2 & 3

SOJOURN

On a path of vengeance, Arwyn makes for Mordath's castle. But how can you kill a man who has already died once and has a troll army at his back? Perhaps with the help of a cunning new ally...

Chapters 16-18

MERIDIAN

Sephie and the Pirates of the Wind continue to harass Cadador's trade routes. However, Ilahn has a plan to crush the resistance and consolidate his power over Meridian.

Chapter 4

CRUX

One hundred thousand years after the sinking of Atlantis, the six Atlanteans to come out of stasis still don't know what happened while they slept. Now they concentrate on trying to revive their friends and loved ones.

(click)

Whoa!

PREQUEL

SCHOLARS WRITE HISTORY IN BOOKS.

WARRIORS WRITE HISTORY IN BLOOD.

Ron
MARZ
WRITER

Bart
SEARS
PENCILER

Mark
PENNINGTON
INKER

Michael
ATIYEH
COLORIST

Dave
LANPHEAR
LETTERER

I am the warlord Tadasi

Now our bloodline leads only to me and to my brother, Nobuyuki.

Though we were both raised in the samurai tradition, Nobuyuki embraced religion and became a monk. It has been years since he was called

to the Emperor Mitsumune himself. The forces of my nation are his sword to wield, but I am the hand that holds the blade.

My comrades in this are not what is expected, but they have spilled blood for me and I have bled with them.

Always to my left is Wulf, an outlander hailing from lands far distant from ours. He is as a mountain, a warrior whose sheer ferocity I have yet to see matched.

To my right is Yamane Aiko, delicate and deadly. I am not fond of the notion of female samurai, but Aiko is any man's equal. She has come to mean more to me than simply a strong sword to match my own.

I would have no others at my side.

Our lives belong to the Emperor Mitsumune, who sits upon the Throne of Petals in his castle at Yazaki.

Mitsumune has been my friend since childhood. We played together as boys. We shared adventures as young men. I love him as I love my own brother.

Of late, though, I begin to wonder if his duties do not tax him too greatly. There are times when he is not the man I know, certainly not the boy whose nose I bloodied as we pretended to be sumo.

*W*here Mitsumune's decisions were once just, now he is ... unpredictable. The whispers at court had already begun when he called me before him and commanded the unthinkable.

*M*itsumune bade me attack the empire of Shinacea, which crouches across the Tsuneo Channel on our western shores like an insatiable beast poised to devour lesser prey.

*N*ayado is a mouse to the great dragon of Shinacea. We are outnumbered a hundred to one. But my Emperor has said that it must be so, and I have no choice but to obey.

I gathered my troops and told them to prepare to conquer the bloated enemy to the west.

I told them they were the finest warriors of any land. I told them their bravery was without peer.

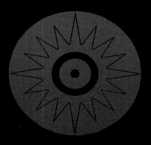

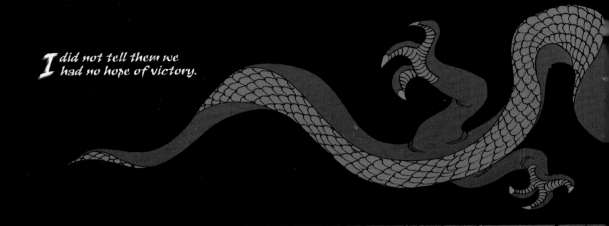

I did not tell them we had no hope of victory.

*W*e attempted a landing upon Shinacea's shores, but found its vast army awaiting us. My warriors were indeed the finest and bravest of any land.

*A*nd still they were slaughtered.

More than half my army perished there, so many that the sea turned to blood. Our losses would have been even greater had I not called the retreat when I did.

So dragging our wounded with us we fled back across the sea, and I prepared to go before my Emperor and pay the price failure demands.

But it seems I will not have that chance. Shinacea's anger was piqued by our arrogance. Their army has followed us across the sea, and now fouls Nayado's soil beneath its boot heels.

The remnants of my soldiers prepare to make a final stand here, on ground that has absorbed the blood of so many battles. These plains are the gateway to Yazaki, and each life that defends it will be dearly sold.

This night I prayed. I lifted pleas to the same gods whom my brother has embraced. I prayed for delivery, so that Nayado might not be wiped from the face of the earth.

And my prayers were answered. A woman unknown to me appeared, a woman possessed of fiery eyes, who set upon my flesh a mark of the gods, a symbol of their favor.

Now, as I wait for the sun to crest the horizon, I am ready to perform my last duty for my Emperor. There is power in this sigil with which I have been graced.

But I do not know if it is the mark of our salvation...

YES, I'M SURE YOU ARE.

WE WANT YOU TO BE A *FAT* LITTLE MOUSE.

MY LORD?

THE DIARY?

YOU DIDN'T SAY HELLO TO MY FRIEND, YUKIO. HE'S A *PLUMP* LITTLE ONE, ISN'T HE?

WHAT A *LUCKY* MOUSE YOU ARE. NO ONE IS ALLOWED WITHIN THESE WALLS SAVE THE EMPEROR HIMSELF.

ARE THESE NOT THE MOST *EXQUISITE* GARDENS IN ALL SHINACEA?

IN ALL THE *WORLD*?

SOMETIMES THE VERY SMALL HAVE *GOOD REASON* TO FEAR THE VERY LARGE.

I HAVE *NEVER* BEEN VERY SMALL.

SO.

TELL ME OF THE COURT OF THE WISE AND KIND EMPEROR MITSUMUNE OF NAYADO.

IS HIS *TONGUE* STILL LOOSE AROUND HIS CONCUBINES?

NAYADO STILL REELS FROM THE DEFEAT OF ITS ARMY.

MY GENERALS *ALSO* TELL ME TALES OF *GODS* DESCENDING FROM THE HEAVENS TO THE BATTLEFIELD.

THEY TELL ME TODOSI WAS *SLAIN* BY ONE OF THESE GODS.

COME, *COME*, MY LITTLE FRIEND.

ALL TRUE?

ALL TRUE, MY LORD, THOUGH EVEN *I* AM NOT CERTAIN WHAT IT ALL MEANS.

EVENTS TOOK A MOST *UNEXPECTED* TURN.

DID THEY? AND HOW COULD *YOU* KNOW OF THINGS THAT OCCUR BEYOND YAZAKI'S WALLS?

MY GENERALS TELL ME VICTORY WAS *OURS*.

SHINACEA'S MIGHT *OVERWHELMED* NAYADO'S DEFENDERS.

AND YET OUR ARMIES FLED BACK ACROSS THE SEA BEFORE WE COULD PRESS A FINAL TRIUMPH.

BEFORE I HELD NAYADO IN MY HANDS.

DON'T BE AFRAID. IT'S ALL RIGHT.

THERE'S A GOOD BOY.

THERE'S A *BRAVE* BOY.

I HAVE MY WAYS, DO I NOT?

DAWN BROUGHT THE BATTLE...

...EVEN BEFORE
THE MORNING
FOG HAD LIFTED.

I SAW
IT ALL.

THE MARK
TODOSI
BORE MADE HIM
THE EQUAL OF
TEN MEN. OF A
HUNDRED MEN.

HE FOUGHT AS
THOUGH HE
WAS DEATH ITSELF
GIVEN FORM.

HIS SWORD LEFT
A WAKE OF
CARNAGE EVERY-
WHERE IT STRUCK.

STIRRED BY THEIR WARLORD'S EXAMPLE, NAYADO'S SONS STRUGGLED FIERCELY, NOT FOR THEIR OWN SURVIVAL BUT FOR THAT OF THEIR ENTIRE NATION.

IT WAS GLORIOUS...

...BUT NOT NEARLY ENOUGH.

SHINACEA'S STRENGTH OF NUMBERS WAS IRRESISTABLE. EACH SOLDIER WHO PERISHED WAS REPLACED BY TWO MORE.

TODOSI REALIZED THE HOPELESSNESS OF THE BATTLE AND FELL TO HIS KNEES IN DESPAIR. HE CRIED OUT TO THE GODS...

...AND THIS TIME THEY APPEARED TO HIM.

HERE YOUR OWN FORCES BROKE RANKS AND RAN, LORD, FEARING AN OPPONENT WHO COULD CALL DOWN THE GODS FROM THEIR HEAVEN.

SUCH WAS THE LOYALTY OF TODOSI'S MEN THAT, THINKING THEIR WARLORD WAS THREATENED, THEY SURGED FORWARD AND ATTACKED THE GODS.

THE GODS SHOWED THEM NO MERCY.

WHEN THE MONK ROSE, HE CARRIED NOT ONLY THE WEAPON OF THE GODS IN HIS HAND...

...BUT ALSO THEIR MARK UPON HIS FLESH, INHERITED FROM HIS BROTHER.

I SAW NOTHING MORE...

...BECAUSE I CAME HERE. TO *YOU*.

THIS WEAPON OF HEAVEN. IS IT *KNOWN* TO YOU?

I HAVE NEVER SEEN ITS LIKE.

BUT IT REMAINS IN THE POSSESSION OF TODOSI'S BROTHER.

THE MONK.

YES...

...THOUGH HE IS A CREATURE OF DUTY. IT SEEMS LIKELY HE WILL PLACE THE WEAPON IN MITSUMUNE'S HANDS.

IF THIS WEAPON IS TRULY AS YOU SAY...

HOW *VERY* FORTUNATE.

...A DIVINE INSTRUMENT CAPABLE OF CAUSING EVEN THE *GODS* TO TREMBLE, IT HARNESSES POWER ENOUGH TO DESTROY *NATIONS*.

I WOULD *CONQUER* NAYADO ONCE AND FOR ALL, BUT I DARE NOT ATTACK WHILE THE WEAPON IS IN THEIR POSSESSION.

HOW *FORTUNATE*, THEN...

...THAT I AM ACQUAINTED WITH SOMEONE SO CLOSE...

...TO NAYADO'S EMPEROR.

I AM MITSUMUNE'S FAVORITE AMONG HIS CONCUBINES.

HE FINDS IT DIFFICULT TO RESIST MY CHARMS...

...BECAUSE I'VE SHOWN HIM *DELIGHTS* HIS MIND CAN SCARCELY IMAGINE.

I SERVE *HIS* PLEASURE...

BAD BUSINESS, MAKING BARGAINS WITH DEMONS.

THEY'RE DANGEROUS AND UNTRUSTWORTHY, LITTLE ONE, EVEN WHEN THEY'RE BEHOLDEN TO YOU.

BUT SUCH BARGAINS ARE A *NECESSARY EVIL* IN ORDER TO MAINTAIN POWER IN AN EMPIRE AS VAST AS SHINACEA.

DESPITE ITS SIZE SHINACEA HAS *MANY* ENEMIES, MANY LESSER FOES WHO ARE JEALOUS OF OUR GRANDEUR AND WOULD SEE IT DESTROYED.

IT HAS *ALWAYS* BEEN SO...

...WE DEVOUR THEM.

...BUT SHINACEA'S MYRIAD ENEMIES HAVE NEVER SUCCEEDED IN *PULLING DOWN* THE EMPIRE.

IT FALLS TO *ME* TO BE VIGILANT. *I MUST KEEP SHINACEA SAFE* FROM ALL THOSE WHO WOULD ATTACK IT.

SO WE ARE PATIENT. WE WATCH OUR FOES CAREFULLY...

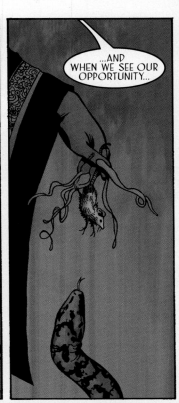

...AND WHEN WE SEE OUR OPPORTUNITY...

NAYADO WILL BE NO DIFFERENT.

Negation™

CHAPTER 1

PELLETIER '01
MEIKIS   JLR

It only took the God-Emperor CHARON ten thousand years to conquer His entire universe and forge the interstellar empire known as:

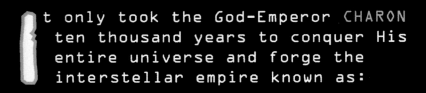

the Negation

But omnipotence isn't enough. Charon now casts His baleful eye across the gulf between realities...

...and He covets the bright and thriving worlds in our cosmos.

At His behest, one hundred ill-fated souls were abducted from scores of our worlds and brought to His dark realm to be tortured and tested... to struggle and die.

Charon watches the grim experiment unfold, cataloguing humanity's strengths and weaknesses, preparing His strategies for the war to come. But, for a prisoner named Obregon Kaine, the war has already begun.

Deep within the stronghold of the enemy, one ordinary man plots the downfall of a god...

KAINE

EVINLEA

JAVI

KOMPTIN

CHARON

TONY BEDARD WITH MARK WAID
WRITERS

PAUL PELLETIER
PENCILER

DAVE MEIKIS
INKER

JAMES ROCHELLE
COLORIST

TROY PETERI
LETTERER

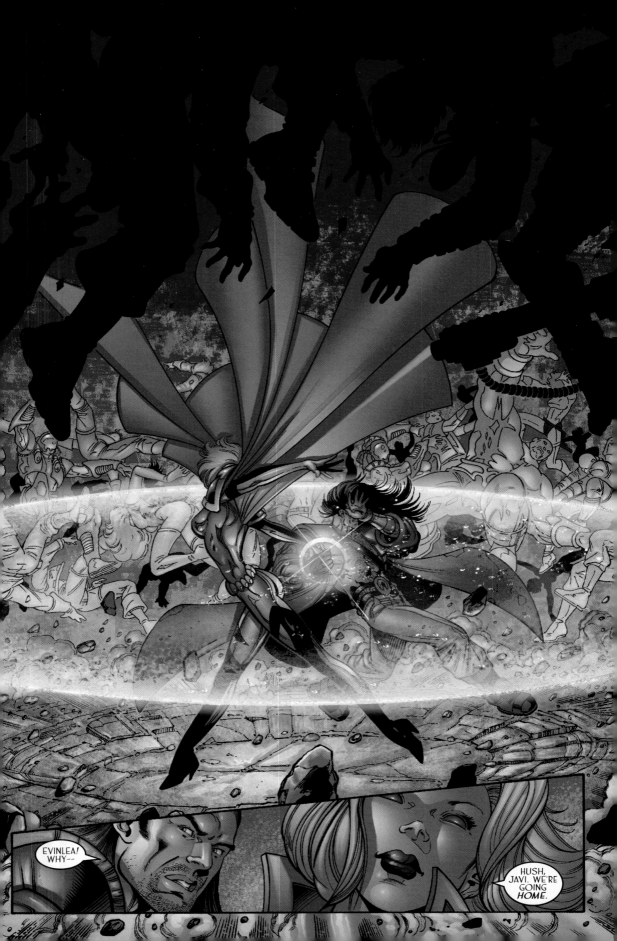

THE NEGATION ALREADY *HAS* A GOD. WE DON'T NEED ANOTHER.

"THOSE WITH THE *MARK* MANIFEST VERY *SPECIFIC* TALENTS. JAVI, FOR EXAMPLE, DOESN'T APPEAR TO WIELD POWER HIMSELF. BUT HE *CAN* AMPLIFY THE ABILITIES OF WHOMEVER HE TOUCHES.

GUARDS, SEPARATE THEM. THROW THE MALE IN SOLITARY.

"WE'RE CURRENTLY TRYING TO DETERMINE WHY HIS MARK WORKS, WHILE SO MANY ARE SCRAMBLED. MAYBE IT'S BECAUSE IT WORKS FOR *OTHERS*."

WHERE WAS I? OH YES: YOUR DAILY *TESTS*. SOME ARE PHYSICAL. SOME ARE COGNITIVE. *ALL* OF THEM CAN KILL YOU.

REFUSE TO PARTICIPATE, OR BREAK THE RULES AND YOU WILL BE EXECUTED.

NOW, GO -- AND EAT HEARTY. YOU'LL NEED YOUR STRENGTH!

"WITH EVINLEA NEUTRALIZED, THERE WERE STILL OTHERS TO WHOM KAINE MIGHT TURN..."

BLORT

"THE *SAURIAN FEMALE*, FOR EXAMPLE, WITH HER STRENGTH, CLAWS AND VENOM."

THIS... IS A CRIME AGAINST NATURE.

"OR *PRISONER IRESS*, WHO IS HALF HUMAN AND HALF FIRST."

"AND THEN THERE'S *PRISONER CORRIN*, WHO APPEARS TO BE OPERATING AT LESS THAN FULL EFFECTIVENESS BECAUSE SHE MISUNDERSTANDS HER SITUATION..."

"SEE, SHE THINKS THIS IS ALL A *BAD DREAM* --THAT SHE'S REALLY SLEEPING IN A STASIS TUBE UNDER THE SEA, ALONG WITH THE REST OF HER KIND.

"THE INMATES JUST THINK SHE'S *CRAZY.*"

...OUR PRISONERS FROM THESE TESTS: THE LIMITS OF THEIR *STRENGTH, SPEED* AND *AGILITY*...

...THEIR *INTELLIGENCE* AND PROBLEM-SOLVING SKILLS...

...THEIR ABILITY TO ENDURE *PAIN*.

TODAY, I PITTED KAINE, THE SAURIAN AND ANOTHER PRISONER AGAINST THREE ATHRANIAN SCOUT-WARRIORS.

THE *RULES* OF THE EXERCISE WERE CLEAR: THIS WAS A *RACE*.

FIRST ONE TO EXIT THE ARENA WOULD GET TO *LIVE*.

AND JUST

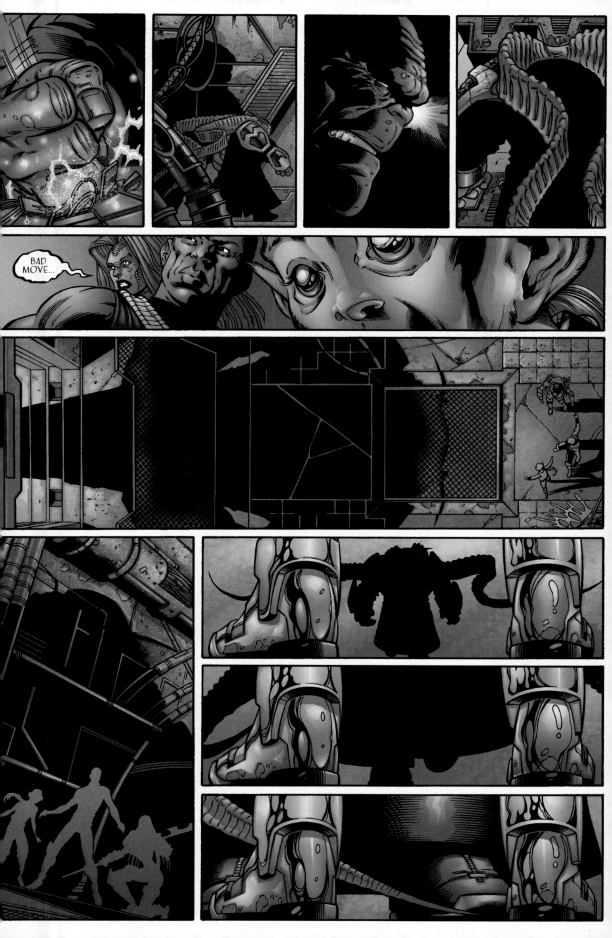

THIS ONE **INTERESTS** ME. HE IS NOT TO BE DESTROYED MERELY TO SATISFY YOUR **ANGER.**

LET THE EXPERIMENT CONTINUE. IF HE SHOULD FALL IN SOME TEST OR SUCCUMB TO AN ACCIDENT, SO BE IT. BUT KNOW THAT I AM WATCHING.

"AND THEN HE WAS GONE."

TEN **THOUSAND** YEARS I'VE SERVED HIM. CONQUERED A **UNIVERSE** FOR HIM.

BUT I HAVE **NEVER** KNOWN EMPEROR CHARON-- BLESSED BE HIS NAME-- TO INTERCEDE LIKE THIS.

ALL FOR SOMETHING AS WORTHLESS AS YOUR **PRIDE!** I'D END YOU MYSELF RIGHT NOW, BUT...

...YOU WERE RIGHT ABOUT **ONE** THING, KOMPTIN: I AM **NOT** STUPID.

THE EMPEROR LEFT YOU AT YOUR POST. FAR BE IT FROM ME TO QUESTION HIS WISDOM.

CARRY ON, AND REMEMBER HIS **WORDS** WELL.

END TRANSMISSION.

Oh, I REMEMBER THEM **PRECISELY.**

LET THE EXPERIMENT CONTINUE. IF HE SHOULD FALL IN SOME TEST...

...OR SUCCUMB TO AN **ACCIDENT...**

...SO BE IT.

NegaTion™

CHAPTER 2

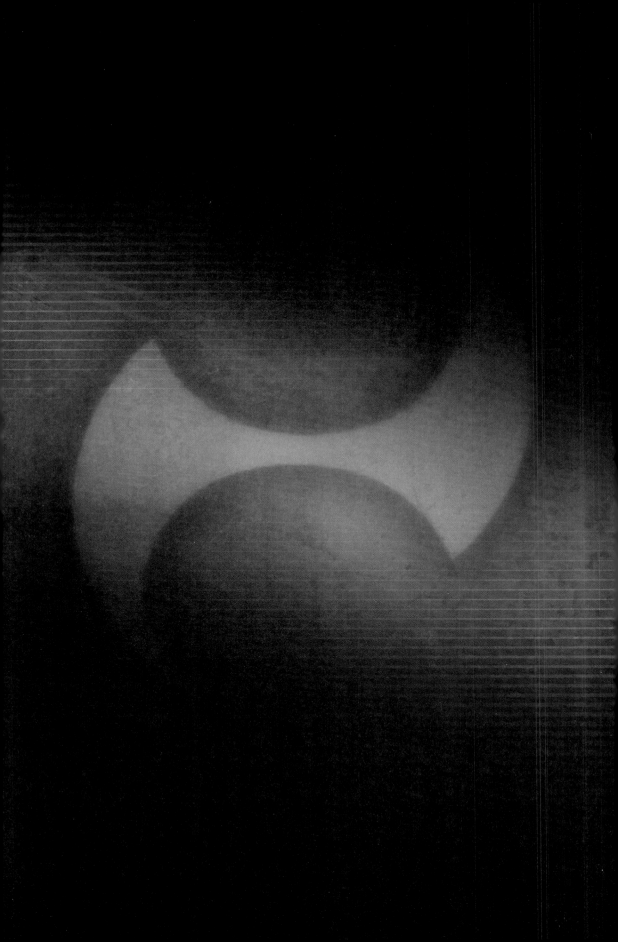

=GASP=

KAINE BASED HIS PLAN ON A RECENT EXPERIENCE HE'D HAD IN THE *TESTING ARENA...*

KOMPTIN STACKED THE DECK AGAINST THE *LIZARD LADY* AND ME.

WHEN WE SURVIVED HIS TEST ANYWAY, HE GOT SO MAD HE CAME DOWN FROM HIS CONTROL ROOM TO FINISH US OFF *HIMSELF.*

HE *WOULD'VE,* TOO. BUT THEN THE DAMNDEST THING HAPPENED...

SOME *GLOWING GUY*-- I THINK HE'S THE *LEADER* OF THIS WHOLE "NEGATION" OUTFIT --STEPPED OUT OF NOWHERE AND *STOPPED* HIM.

BUT THAT'S ANOTHER MATTER. MY POINT IS THAT IT TOOK KOMPTIN LESS THAN A MINUTE TO WALK FROM HIS CONTROL CENTER TO THE ARENA FLOOR.

WHICH MEANS THAT IF WE CAN *BREACH* THE ARENA WALL, HE SHOULD BE *RIGHT THERE*--AND WE CAN TAKE HIM *HOSTAGE.*

HE MUST HAVE A *TRANSPORT SHIP* PARKED SOMEWHERE IN THIS PLACE. WE'LL STEAL IT AND FLY IT *OUT* OF HERE.

AND WHAT OF YOUR GLOWING MAN? WILL HE NOT JUST STOP US THE MOMENT WE GET TOO FAR?

IF HE'S REALLY THE EMPEROR, HE'S *GOTTA* BE A BUSY GUY. I DOUBT HE'S *ALWAYS* WATCHING.

WE'LL JUST HAVE TO CHANCE IT, AND HOPE THAT ONCE WE'RE OUT OF THE PRISON, HE CAN'T TRACK US.

"KAINE WARNED US THAT THE WARDEN WOULD NOT EASILY BE TAKEN. FOR ADDITIONAL POWER, HE RECRUITED THE OTHER *SIGIL-BEARERS*."

MERCER *DRAKE*, RIGHT? LET ME INTRODUCE YOU TO --

SHASSA. WE'VE MET. ONE OF THE FIRST THINGS I DID WAS COMPARE NOTES WITH ANYONE ELSE WHO BORE THE *MARK*...

...AND WE'RE *NOTHING* ALIKE. HE'S A *CRIMINAL.* I'M A CONSTABLE--

WE'RE *ALL* JAILBIRDS HERE, DRAKE. I HAVE A *PROPOSITION* FOR YOU...

"ON MATUA'S WORLD THEY HAVE DEVISED REMARKABLE METHODS TO MANIPULATE THE *UNIVERSAL ENERGIES* THAT SWIRL AND EDDY UNSEEN ACROSS THE UNIVERSE.

"WHAT MY PEOPLE DO NATURALLY, HIS CALL *MAGIC*.

WITH THE RIGHT WORDS AND GESTURES--AND SOME MENTAL GYMNASTICS-- YOU CAN CAUSE THE *IMPOSSIBLE* TO HAPPEN.

IT TAKES *PRACTICE*, BUT WHEN YOU DO IT RIGHT, IT FEELS A LITTLE LIKE DOING *LONG DIVISION* IN YOUR HEAD.

IT'S JUST A GUESS, BUT I THINK YOU ALL ACCESS THE SAME POWER I DO. THE PROBLEM IS, ON *THIS* WORLD, THE ENERGIES THEMSELVES FEEL SOMEHOW... *CORRUPTED*.

POP

I THINK IN TIME, YOU'LL ALL NATURALLY ADAPT. BUT MAYBE I CAN HELP YOU *CUT* THE ADJUSTMENT PERIOD DOWN TO A FEW DAYS.

"I WOULD'VE LIKED TO HAVE HEARD MORE, BUT OUR *JAILER* SEEMED ALWAYS A STEP AHEAD OF US."

ATTENTION! THE FOLLOWING PRISONERS WILL REPORT TO THE TESTING ARENA IMMEDIATELY!

PRISONERS HALPRIN, FINNEY, HUMM...AND *THALIA*. THE REST OF YOU: AS YOU WERE.

NO! WE'RE NOT *READY* YET--!

IT'S ALRIGHT, MATUA...LET ME GO.

WE'D HAVE TO ANYWAY. WHATEVER POWER MIGHT STILL BE IN HER, THE WOMAN'S *BLIND*. SHE'S *USELESS*.

MY FRIEND IS NOT *DISPOSABLE*. I'M *NOT* LETTING HER GO. WE'LL DO THIS *RIGHT HERE*, *RIGHT NOW*.

NO! IF WE DON'T STRIKE INSIDE THE *ARENA*, THEN IT'S ALL FOR NOTHING.

JUST...JUST *WAIT* HERE. LET ME GET INTO THE ARENA. WHEN YOU HEAR MY *SIGNAL*, FIGHT YOUR WAY OUT OF HERE AND COME *RUNNING*.

DO YOU *UNDERSTAND* WHAT I'M TELLING YOU?

...

YES... I'LL TELL THE OTHERS TO BE READY.

I'M SORRY, MATUA, BUT YOU CAN'T AVOID *SACRIFICE* IF YOU'RE FIGHTING A *WAR*.

AND SO, ON THALIA'S SIGNAL, WE STORMED THE ARENA--

=UNH=

ARE YOU OKAY?

YEAH...

...BUT...WHERE *IS* THALIA? WHAT WAS HER SIGNAL?

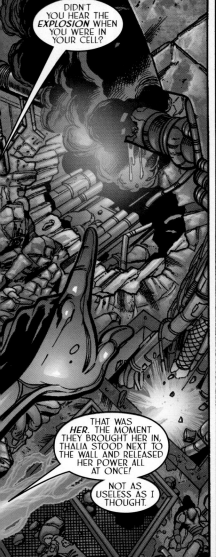

DIDN'T YOU HEAR THE *EXPLOSION* WHEN YOU WERE IN YOUR CELL?

THAT WAS *HER*. THE MOMENT THEY BROUGHT HER IN, THALIA STOOD NEXT TO THE WALL AND RELEASED HER POWER ALL AT ONCE!

NOT AS USELESS AS I THOUGHT.

EVERYONE! TO THE SPACEPORT!

"KAINE *FORCED* OUR JAILER TO CONCENTRATE HIS GUARDS AROUND THE ARENA, LEAVING THE WAY OPEN TO OUR *TRUE* OBJECTIVES:

"WHILE EVERYONE ELSE MADE THE ARENA ASSAULT LOOK *CONVINCING*, HE SENT ME TO FREE *YOU*...

"...AND KAINE HIMSELF TOOK A FEW OTHERS TO LOCATE THE *SPACEPORT.*"

TAKE WESTIN AND MAKE SURE HE CAN *DRIVE* THAT THING!

I'LL *JOIN* YOU AS SOON AS THE *OTHERS* ARRIVE!

WHAT DO YOU *MEAN*, PRISONER JAVI ESCAPED?! WHAT IN THE NAME OF CHARON IS *GOING ON* AROUND HERE?!

THAT'S WHAT *I'D* LIKE TO KNOW, HIGH CASTELLAN.

GENERAL KRYZORR! WE'RE EXPERIENCING A LITTLE *SETBACK* HERE--

YOU'VE *LOST CONTROL*, KOMPTIN. AND THAT'S SOMETHING WE CANNOT AFFORD.

WE CAN'T HAVE SO MANY OF THEIR TOP ASSETS RUNNING LOOSE IN NEGATION SPACE.

I'M PULLING THE PLUG ON THIS FACILITY. YOU ARE HEREBY RELIEVED OF DUTY.

NO! I CAN STILL *STOP* THEM! GENERAL, *PLEASE--!*

ATTENTION ALL PERSONNEL! EXTINCTION WAVE ARMED! EVACUATE FACILITY IMMEDIATELY!

EXTINCTION WAVE DEPLOYING! EVACUATE IMMEDIATELY!

EVINLEA...

GET IN THE SHIP, JAVI. NOW.

IMPACT IN THREE MINUTES!

EXTINCTION WAVE IMPACT IN THIRTY SECONDS!

THE WRONG PEOPLE ESCAPED. ARE YOU *SATISFIED?*

JUST LEMME THINK...

THAT *THING* YOU GRABBED THE SHIP WITH. IT'S LIKE A *FORCE-FIELD*, RIGHT?

CAN YOU...

CAN YOU PICK UP A WHOLE SECTION OF THIS PRISON AND...I DON'T KNOW...

...*WRAP* IT IN SOME KIND OF FORCE-*BUBBLE?*

FLY IT INTO SPACE...?

I COULD TELEPORT US *ALL* TO ANOTHER WORLD-- *IF* I KNEW WHERE ONE WAS AROUND HERE!

JUST *ANSWER* ME!

CAN YOU FLY US UP AND BRING ALONG SOMETHING TO BREATHE?

YES! BUT *NOT EVERYONE!* AND FOR *HOW LONG?* DO YOU HAVE *ANY* IDEA HOW *IMMENSE* SPACE IS?

YOU GOT A *BETTER* IDEA?

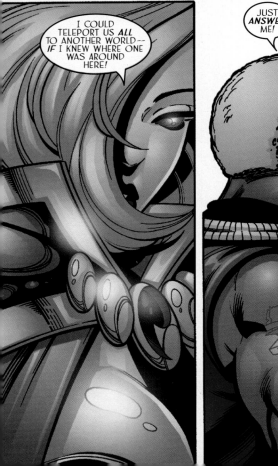

...QUIT...→NFF←...STRUGGLING...

FIVE SECONDS!

FOUR!

THREE!

MY WORD OF *HONOR:* I SHALL NOT FORSAKE YOU.

TWO!

ONE!

PFFT

I'M SORRY, MATUA, BUT YOU CAN'T AVOID *SACRIFICE* IF YOU'RE FIGHTING A *WAR.*

BOHICA...

Our Story So Far...

Mordath

Ayden

Arwyn

Darkness spread across the Five Lands as the dread warlord Mordath placed nearly all of Quin under his booted heel. Just as hope was nearly extinguished, a warrior calling himself Ayden gathered the survivors of Mordath's depredations and forged an army that defeated Mordath's troll forces. Ayden slew Mordath, piercing him with an arrow.

Offered sovereignty over the Five Lands, Ayden declined, preferring to retreat to the solitude from which he'd come. However, before departing, Ayden broke the fatal arrow into Five Fragments and scattered them to the Five Lands, promising to return should the pieces ever be reunited.

That was three hundred years ago. Now Mordath has risen from the grave and conquered all that lies before him. The last city to fall before his armies was Gerrindor. The city itself was burned to the ground, its inhabitants put to the sword. One woman survived, and swore vengeance for the deaths of her husband and daughter.

Her name is Arwyn.

Ron MARZ WRITER   **Greg LAND** PENCILER   **Drew GERACI** INKER   **Caesar RODRIGUEZ** COLORIST   **Troy PETERI** LETTERER

THIS IS AS FAR AS YOU GO, KREEG. I HAVE TO DO SOMETHING AND I WON'T BE...

...I DON'T KNOW WHEN I'LL BE BACK. *YOU* CAN'T COME.

WHAT'S *THAT* ABOUT?

SO YOU... TAKE CARE OF YOURSELF, BOY.

I LOVE YOU.

WFF

KREEG, *NO.*

YOU'RE NOT SUPPOSED TO FOLLOW.

STAY, KREEG.

Mordath is the most powerful being on all of Quin.

Powerful enough that only the mad would think themselves capable of destroying him.

GHLK!

HRR!

Of course, only the mad would seek to accomplish the deed...

"DINNER."

...by stealing into his fortress.

Alone.

My own visits to Mordath's fortress have never been undertaken willingly.

It's a vast edifice, as much a symbol of evil as the blood-red banners his troops carry into battle.

It rests upon the same plain in Middelyn once occupied by Mordath's original castle.

That one was torn down piece by piece following his death, the stones cast into the sea.

Upon his return Mordath had it rebuilt, and topped by a tower burning with a great flame fueled by his fiery power.

The beacon can be seen from great distances, a constant reminder of Mordath's rule.

WHO ARE—

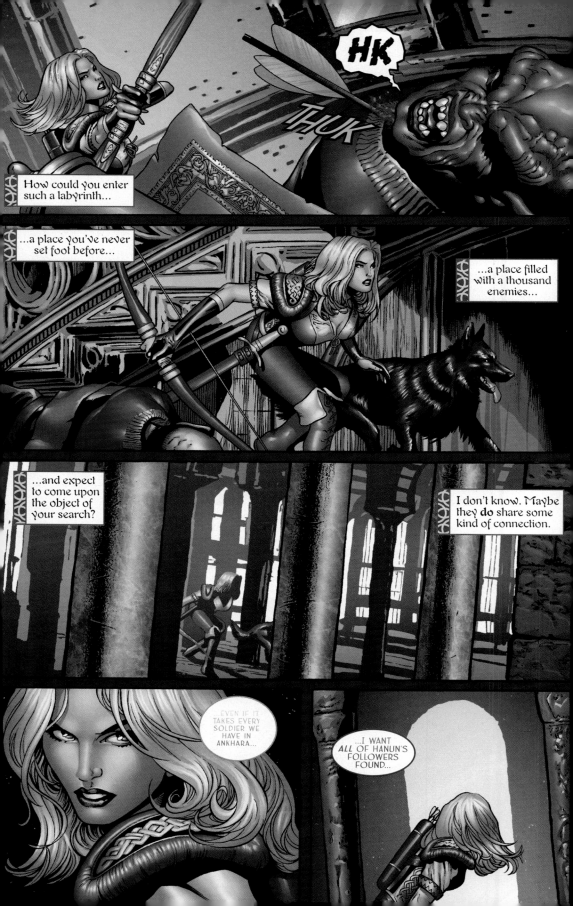

It's said he can't die.

His trolls believe it, certainly.

They believe that having slipped death's embrace once, Mordath can never be reclaimed by it.

I tend to take the opposing view. He was killed once. Why not again?

But then I've always been an optimist.

NO...

KILL HER...

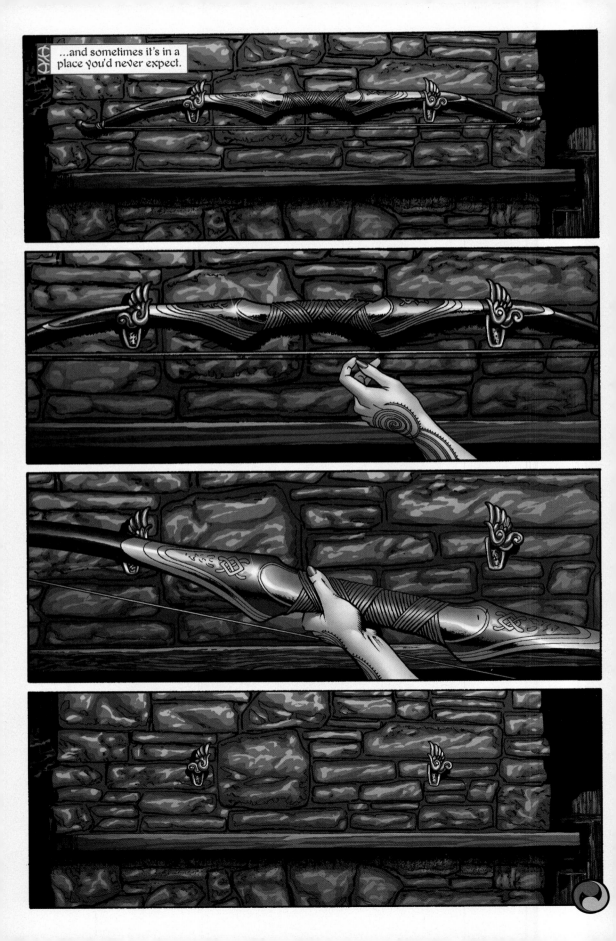

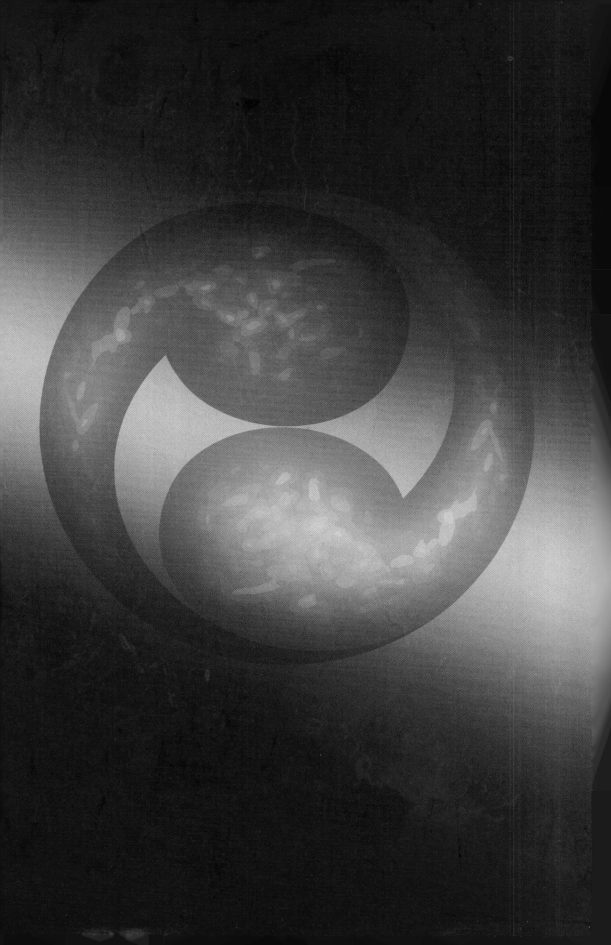

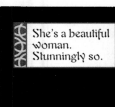

She's a beautiful woman. Stunningly so.

HELLO?

And yet she acts as if the thought never crosses her mind, as if she's not even aware of it.

HELLO, CAN YOU HEAR ME?

Or maybe it's just that she doesn't care.

NNNH...

...HNN?!

NO, NO, LOOK *THIS* WAY...

But it's impossible not to see it...

WAIT! MY *DOG*. WHERE'S MY *DOG*?

I'M GOING TO GUESS AND SAY *THAT'S* HIM OVER THERE...

...THOUGH I THINK THE TROLLS HAVE HIM EARMARKED FOR TONIGHT'S STEW.

TROLLS DON'T HAVE TERRIBLY DISCERNING PALATES, IN CASE YOU WERE WONDERING.

WELCOME TO MORDATH'S DUNGEONS. THE ACCOMMODATIONS ARE FILTHY, BUT THE CUISINE IS WORSE.

I'M *GARETH*.

YOU'LL HAVE TO FORGIVE ME FOR NOT SHAKING YOUR HAND.

WHY HAVEN'T THEY KILLED ME? MORDATH SAID HE WANTED ME KILLED.

I'M NOT EVEN SURE WHY THEY HAVEN'T KILLED *ME*...

...BUT THE TROLLS TEND NOT TO BE TERRIBLY CHATTY.

I CAME HERE TO *KILL* MORDATH.

SHNK

SHNK

YOU WOULDN'T BE THE FIRST.

LISTEN, YANKING ON THOSE CHAINS ISN'T GOING TO DO YOU ANY GOOD, BUT I'VE GOT A—

HANG ON...

...WE'RE ABOUT TO HAVE COMPANY.

YOU'RE WONDERING, I SUPPOSE...

AS I SAID...

...YOU'RE WONDERING WHY YOU'RE ALIVE.

YOU KILLED MY *FAMILY*, YOU BASTARD!

YOU BURNED MY *CITY!*

YOU TOOK AWAY EVERY REASON I HAD TO *LIVE* AND I SWEAR I'LL SEE YOU *DEAD* FOR IT!

I DON'T KNOW WHO YOU ARE.

I DON'T CARE.

YOU CREPT INTO MY CASTLE TRULY BELIEVING YOU COULD KILL ME. SUCH AN AUDACIOUS ACT.

I DIED *ONCE*. IT'S NOT AN EXPERIENCE I INTEND TO REPEAT.

YOU'RE ALIVE BECAUSE I THOUGHT BETTER OF *WASTING* YOUR DEATH. YOU PRESENT AN OPPORTUNITY FOR ME TO IMPART A LESSON TO THE FIVE LANDS.

AS PROPER REWARD FOR YOUR AUDACITY, YOU'LL BE *BURNED* IN A VERY PUBLIC EXECUTION. AND WHEN YOUR PYRE HAS GUTTERED OUT...

...SO WILL THE LAST BIT OF *DEFIANCE* ON QUIN.

PTUH

I SAID, "I'M SORRY." ABOUT YOUR FAMILY.

I CAN'T IMAGINE ANYTHING MORE TERRIBLE.

Oh...

...THANK YOU.

MY NAME IS *ARWYN*.

I LIVE IN GERRINDOR. *LIVED.*

WE HOPED THE CITY MIGHT BE SPARED BECAUSE IT WAS ON THE NORTHERN BORDER, AND THERE WAS NO OPEN REBELLION TO MORDATH'S RULE.

BUT MORDATH DOESN'T ALLOW *ANYTHING* TO ESCAPE HIS GRASP, DOES HE? SO THE TROLLS SWEPT INTO GERRINDOR.

I THINK I MIGHT BE THE ONLY SURVIVOR.

KREEG IS ALL I HAVE LEFT.

I'VE HAD HIM SINCE MY HUSBAND GAVE HIM TO ME AS A PUPPY.

WHY ARE *YOU* HERE?

USING ONE TOO MANY TROLLS FOR TARGET PRACTICE.

BUT I DON'T PLAN ON *STAYING* HERE.

WHAT DO YOU MEAN?

THIS. I TOOK IT OFF ONE OF THE DIMMER GUARDS...

...WHICH DOESN'T NARROW IT DOWN MUCH, I KNOW...

...BUT IT'S FAIRLY USELESS TO *ONE* PERSON. SEE? I CAN'T REACH THE OTHER MANACLE.

BUT WITH *TWO* PEOPLE...

KLAK

HERE.

HURRY UP, THE TROLLS ARE LIABLE TO COME BACK AT ANY TIME.

KLAK

HUMAN! HOW DID YOU—

Ah

THE THINGS I DO...

NNF

...FOR SOMEBODY I JUST *MET*.

HHK!

GRGL!

ARWYN? DON'T TAKE THIS THE WRONG WAY, BUT...

...WHAT ARE YOU *THINKING?!*

NO OFFENSE...

I'M ENJOYING THIS *SO* MUCH MORE THAN BEING IN THE DUNGEON!

CAN'T GET MUCH BETTER, CAN IT?

CHASED THROUGH THE CASTLE OF AN UNDEAD EVIL TYRANT, A HORDE OF TROLLS AT MY HEELS, A DOG AND A MADWOMAN FOLLOWING ME...

...AND *SHE'S* GOT THE DAMN BOW.

COME ON, MAYBE THIS WAY...

...OR *NOT.*

HRAAAA

SHUKT

NOT *GOOD*, ARWYN! TROLLS IN FRONT OF US, TROLLS BEHIND US!

GYAA!

HOW IN AYDEN'S NAME DO WE GET *OUT* OF THIS PLACE?!

WE TRY *THERE!*

GRRFF

THUK

LAST ARROW.

APPARENTLY *THIS* IS WHERE WE MAKE OUR STAND.

AT LEAST WE GOT TO ENJOY THE VIEW.

Meeting her changed my life.

I WANT THE GIRL.

Heh.

Maybe it's changed hers a little as well.

Huh?

Still, back then I was fairly certain the extent of our relationship would be dying together.

WHAT...

MERIDIAN™

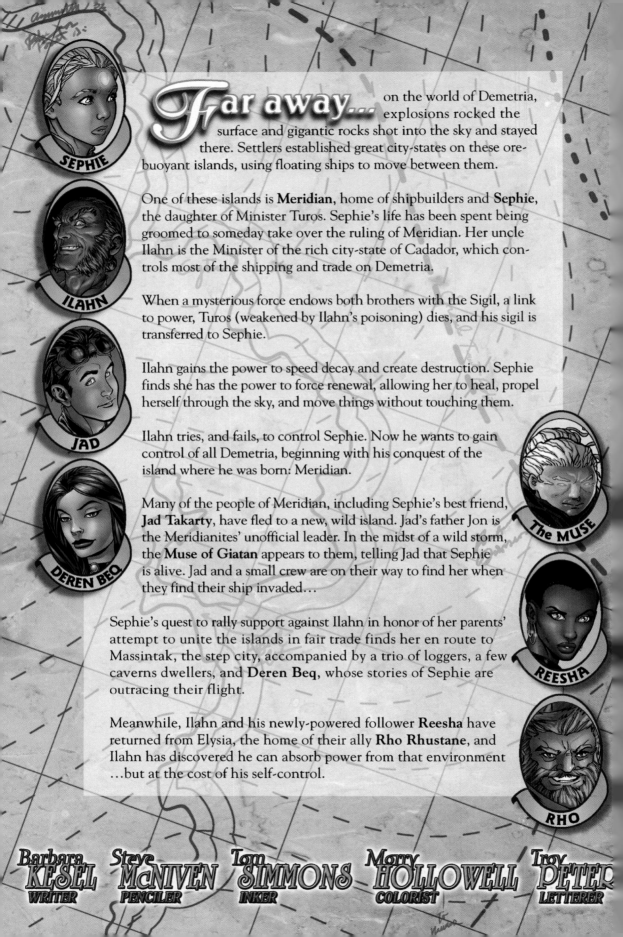

Far away... on the world of Demetria, explosions rocked the surface and gigantic rocks shot into the sky and stayed there. Settlers established great city-states on these ore-buoyant islands, using floating ships to move between them.

One of these islands is **Meridian**, home of shipbuilders and **Sephie**, the daughter of Minister Turos. Sephie's life has been spent being groomed to someday take over the ruling of Meridian. Her uncle Ilahn is the Minister of the rich city-state of Cadador, which controls most of the shipping and trade on Demetria.

When a mysterious force endows both brothers with the Sigil, a link to power, Turos (weakened by Ilahn's poisoning) dies, and his sigil is transferred to Sephie.

Ilahn gains the power to speed decay and create destruction. Sephie finds she has the power to force renewal, allowing her to heal, propel herself through the sky, and move things without touching them.

Ilahn tries, and fails, to control Sephie. Now he wants to gain control of all Demetria, beginning with his conquest of the island where he was born: Meridian.

Many of the people of Meridian, including Sephie's best friend, **Jad Takarty**, have fled to a new, wild island. Jad's father Jon is the Meridianites' unofficial leader. In the midst of a wild storm, the **Muse of Giatan** appears to them, telling Jad that Sephie is alive. Jad and a small crew are on their way to find her when they find their ship invaded…

Sephie's quest to rally support against Ilahn in honor of her parents' attempt to unite the islands in fair trade finds her en route to Massintak, the step city, accompanied by a trio of loggers, a few caverns dwellers, and **Deren Beq**, whose stories of Sephie are outracing their flight.

Meanwhile, Ilahn and his newly-powered follower **Reesha** have returned from Elysia, the home of their ally **Rho Rhustane**, and Ilahn has discovered he can absorb power from that environment …but at the cost of his self-control.

SEPHIE

ILAHN

JAD

DEREN BEQ

The MUSE

REESHA

RHO

Barbara **KESEL** WRITER

Steve **McNIVEN** PENCILER

Tom **SIMMONS** INKER

Morry **HOLLOWELL** COLORIST

Troy **PETER** LETTERER

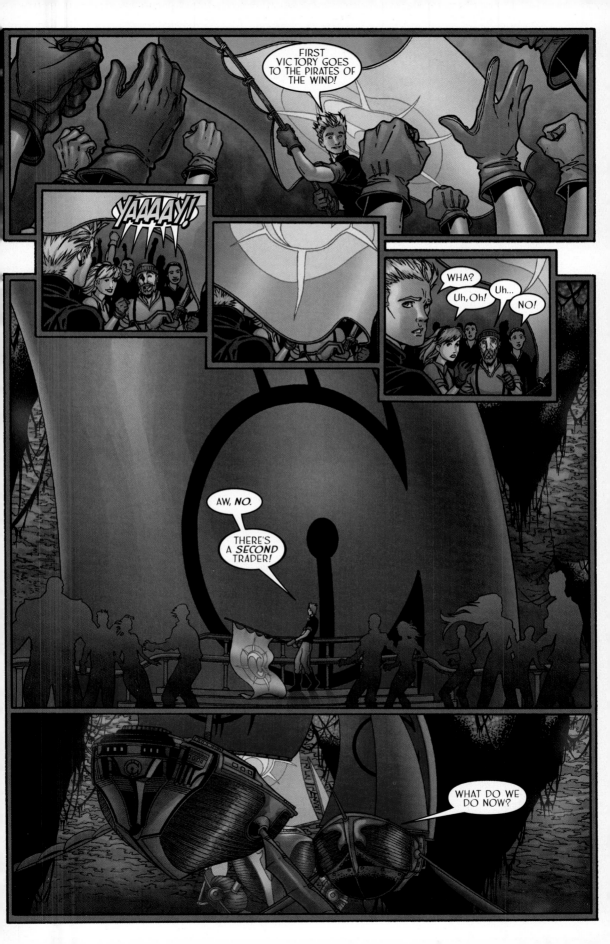

I'LL NEED TO SEE ILAHN ALONE.

BOSCAU...

INFORM MINISTER ILAHN THAT I HAVE AN IMPORTANT COMMUNICATION FOR HIM...

...FROM HIS NIECE.

BUT HIS NIECE IS DEAD, CAPTAIN PATGIEN. SURELY *YOU* HAVEN'T FORGOTTEN...

...Oh.

YOUR ARM.

THE GIRL'S DOING.

WAIT HERE, PLEASE.

I'LL INFORM THE MINISTER.

SO IT'S TRUE.

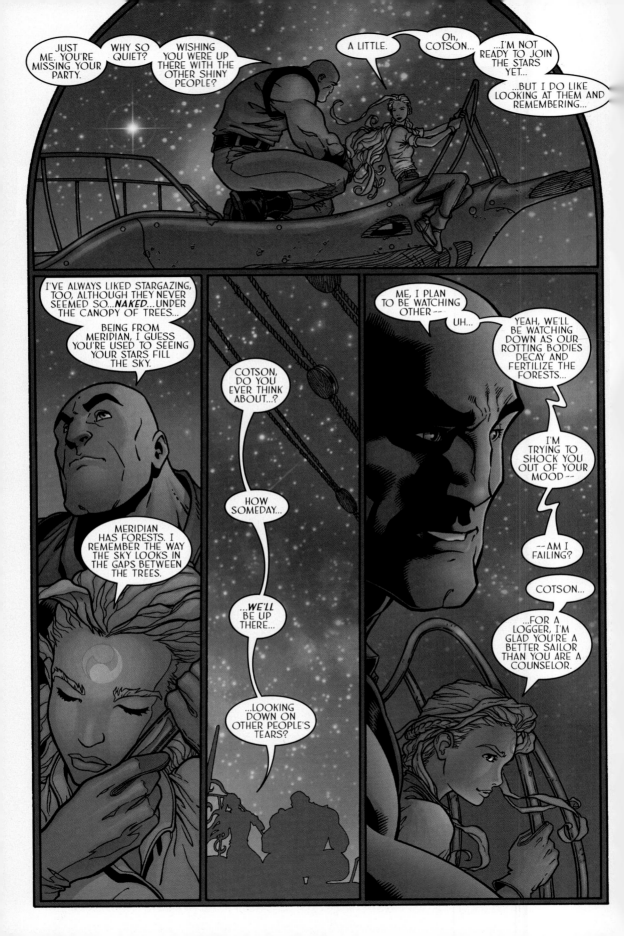

"...THAT MERIDIAN ITSELF BE THE FIRST WEAPON IN MY WAR AGAINST HER MINISTER."

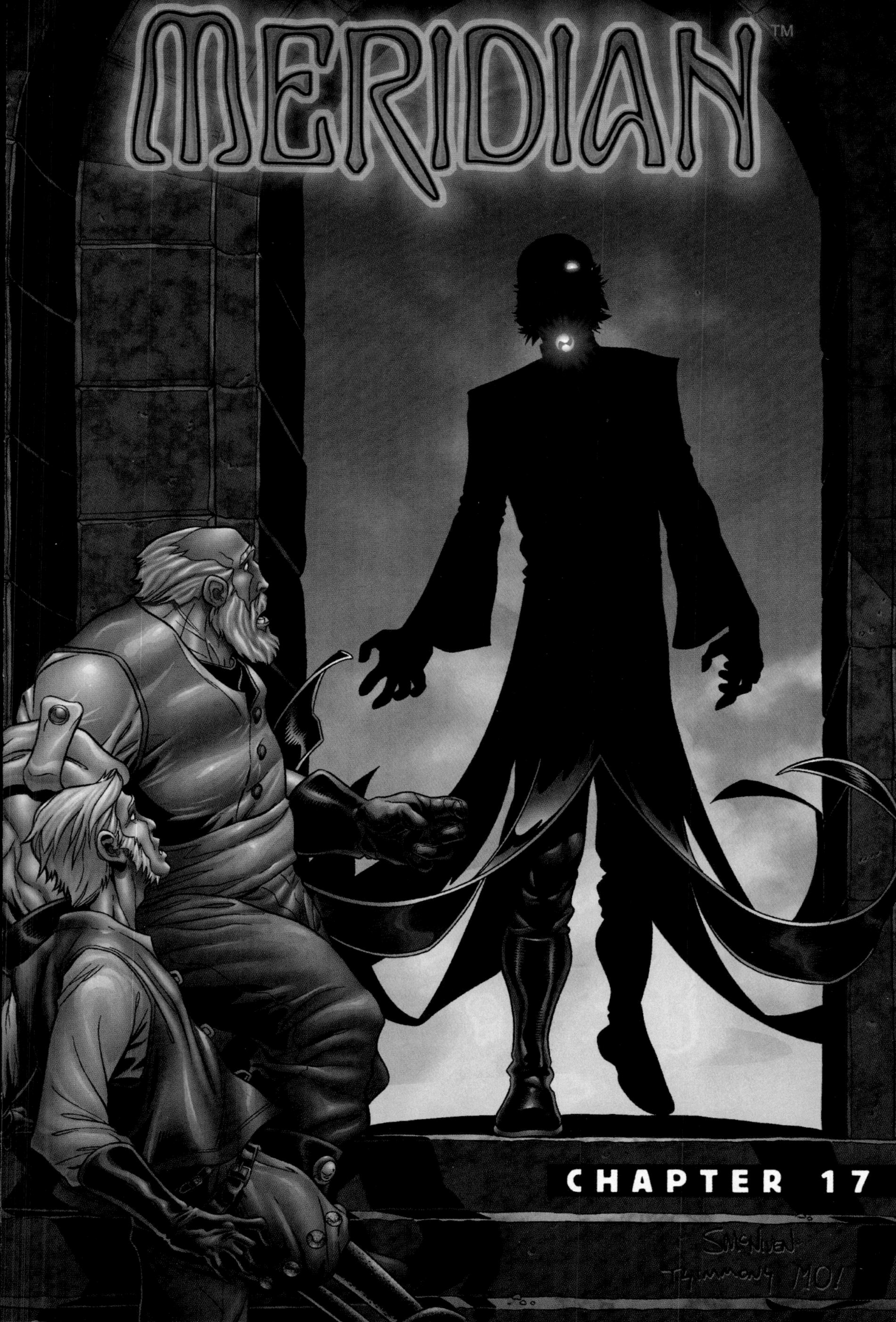
MERIDIAN™
CHAPTER 17

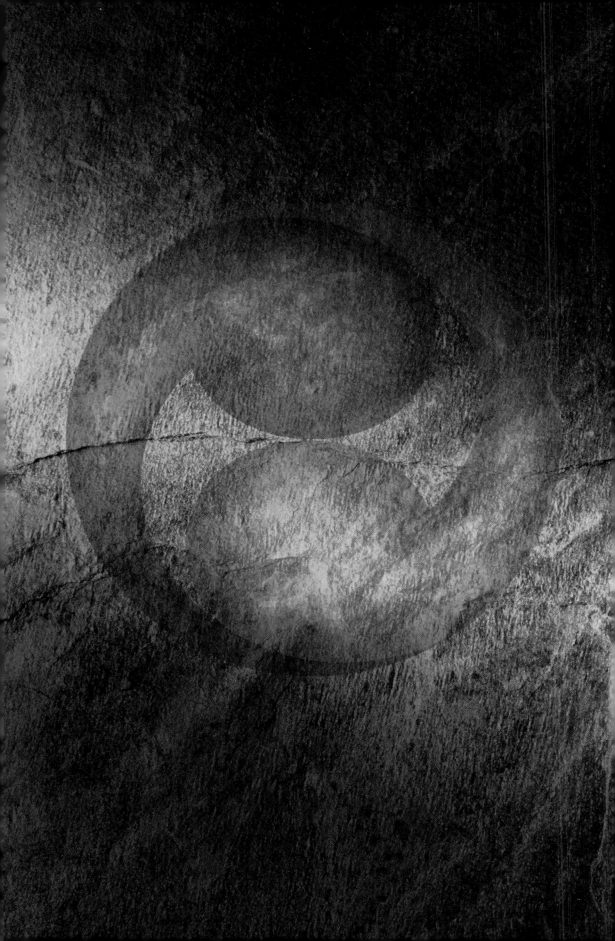

We traveled there to meet our newest allies...

...and to thank them for coming to our rescue.

HULLO! I'M SEPHIE.

I'M--

AH, I KNOW WHO *YOU* ARE.

WORD HAS REACHED US OF THE FLYING MINISTER OF MERIDIAN AND HER EFFORTS TO DEVELOP A NEW TRADE CARTEL.

A FASCINATING DISRUPTION OF ILAHN'S CURRENT MONOPOLY, I'D ADD.

I'M *WYNTREN.* I COORDINATE OUR STUDIES HERE.

THIS IS *NAUK.* HE PROVIDES MY MOBILITY.

WELCOME TO MASSINTAK.

I HEAR OUR NEW SHIPS AIDED YOUR EFFORTS?

INCREDIBLY SO!

THANK YOU SO MUCH--

YOUR SMALL DARTERS -- I'VE NEVER *SEEN* SUCH MANEUVERABILITY, AND I'M FROM *MERIDIAN!*

BUT *YOUR* SHIPS ARE WORKS OF ART.

OURS ARE LITTLE MORE THAN THE PHYSICAL EMBODIMENT OF SCIENTIFIC PRINCIPLE.

WE'RE CONSTANTLY SEEKING OUT NEW CHALLENGES AND YOUR AUDACIOUS ACTIONS HAVE PROVIDED US WITH A NEW ONE!

I'M DELIGHTED TO BE INVOLVED--

WE DO LOTS OF *THINKING* HERE, BUT THERE'S NOT ALWAYS AN OUTLET FOR THE *DOING*.

YET YOU'RE *ALWAYS* DOING.

DREYAN! WELCOME!

LADY WYNTREN, MY LADY MINISTER-- *PLEASED*.

DREYAN?

YOU'RE THE *MINISTER* OF MASSINTAK.

IN NAME ONLY.

WYNTREN'S INSTITUTE HAS ALL BUT ELIMINATED THE TRADITIONAL WAYS.

PROGRESS...

...WE MUST ALWAYS SEEK IT OUT.

THE WORLD IS CONSTANTLY CHANGING AND WE MUST MEET ITS SPEED.

THAT'S WHAT *WE'RE* TRYING TO DO-- CHANGE THE WORLD.

IT'S ABOUT TIME SOMEBODY SHOOK UP OLD ILAHN'S COMFORTABLE LITTLE RACKET.

I'M PROUD TO BE ABLE TO SUPPLY YOU WITH SOME MUSCLE.

I APPRECIATE IT.

ARE ALL THESE BUILDINGS FOR NEW SHIPS?

OH, NO. WE COVER ALL THE SCIENCES: MATHEMATICS, CHEMISTRY, MECHANICS...

WE COULD BE FURTHER ALONG IN OUR EXPERIMENTS, BUT MASSINTAK'S SCIENTIFIC RESEARCH HAS BEEN CRIPPLED BY ILAHN'S TARIFFS AND RESTRICTIONS.

AH, HE HAS ENSURED THAT THE PRICE OF PROGRESS IS TOO STEEP.

IF WE WERE FREE TO SHOW WHAT WE COULD REALLY ACCOMPLISH, YOU'D SEE BETTER INNOVATIONS THAN JUST OUR LITTLE AIR FIGHTERS.

BY THE WAY, I'D LOVE THE OPPORTUNITY TO RUN SOME TESTS ON THAT UNIQUE PROPULSION METHOD YOU EMPLOY.

ME?

THE GIRL'S NOT A NEW TOY, WYNTREN...

...JUST AS MASSINTAK'S NOT JUST *TINKERERS*.

But my fears had to be put aside while we saw to the task at hand--disrupting Ilahn's trade.

It became almost easy-- take over trade ships and then let them continue on their way (sending some of the crew from our two commandeered ships home on each ship)...

...having learned that Ilahn couldn't protect them from us.

WE RULE THE SKIES IN DEFIANCE OF CADADOR'S INEFFECTIVE PROTECTION!

"ILAHN CAN NO LONGER GUARANTEE YOUR SAFE PASSAGE!

SO GO HOME TO YOUR PEOPLE AND ASK THEM IF THEY'D LIKE TO BE FREE OF ILAHN'S RESTRICTIONS --

--AND IF THEY'RE WILLING TO HELP PAY THE PRICE OF THAT FREEDOM BY JOINING US.

Then the same speech, over and over...

ATTENTION, CAPTAIN FROM FALGRIFF!

"YOU ARE UNDER THE CONTROL OF THE PIRATES OF THE WIND!"

"WE'RE CREATING A NEW COALITION OF TRADING STATES, ONE THAT WILL TREAT ALL CITIES FAIRLY--"

I wish I could say my mind was always on my mission...

...but it kept wandering back to...the future...of Meridian.

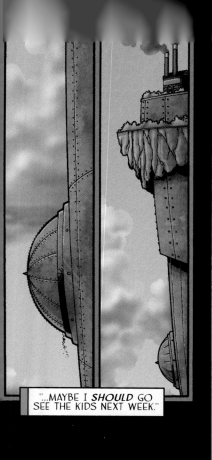
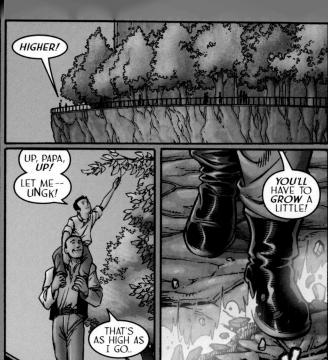

Success was clearly favoring us!

We'd gained so many allies so quickly, my beautiful new ship was bursting at the seams...

...so much so that I had to LEAVE it to find the room to think!

LOOK AT YOU...

GMMF!

TAKE HIM BELOW.

MERIDIAN™

CHAPTER 18

Chapter 18
By

Barbara
KESEL
WRITER

Derec
AUCOIN
ILLUSTRATOR

Jason
LAMBERT
COLORIST

Troy
PETERI
LETTERER

The Pirates of the Wind--a romantic name for the unromantic trials of working to change our world's only system of trade.

Uncle Ilahn may have had time for news of our blockades to reach him in Cadador...

...but the engineers of Massintak had also had time to apply their enthusiasm to the challenges of piracy. By adapting sails to fit sailors, they allowed us a safer form of boarding...

...one every sailor was eager to test.

Today I wasn't the only one to fly.

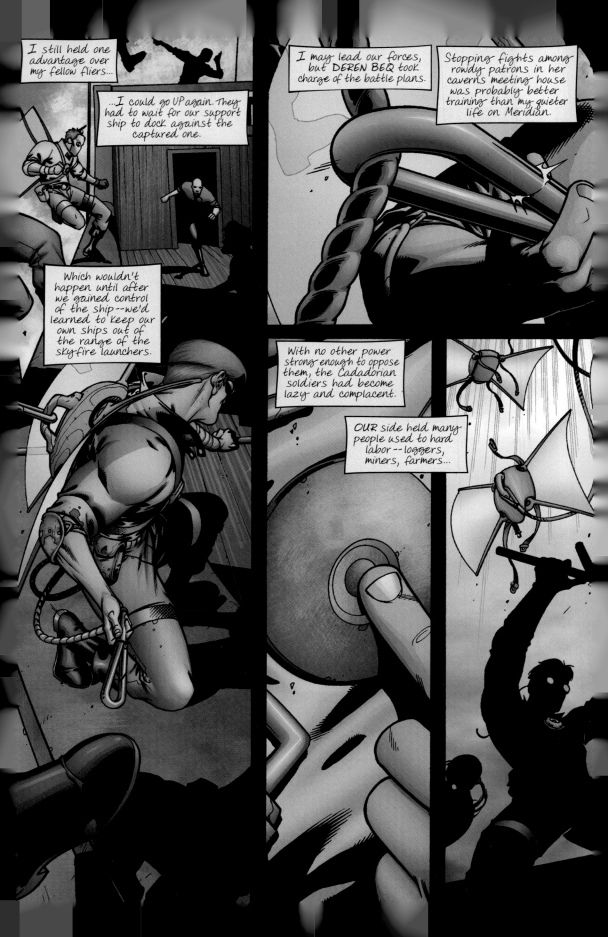

I still held one advantage over my fellow fliers...

...I could go UP again. They had to wait for our support ship to dock against the captured one.

Which wouldn't happen until after we gained control of the ship--we'd learned to keep our own ships out of the range of the skyfire launchers.

I may lead our forces, but DEREN BEQ took charge of the battle plans.

Stopping fights among rowdy patrons in her caverns meeting house was probably better training than my quieter life on Meridian.

With no other power strong enough to oppose them, the Cadadorian soldiers had become lazy and complacent.

OUR side held many people used to hard labor--loggers, miners, farmers...

Taking their ship proved to be simple.

...and quite a few who viewed brawling as recreation.

Which meant the biggest danger our fighters faced...

...was an accident if they forgot to reattach their safety lines after detaching them from the portable sails.

HEY, SEPHIE.

YOU'RE DOING GREAT, JAD.

THINK SO?

UH, SEPH--

WHEN THIS IS OVER, CAN WE FIND A SPOT TO TALK... JUST US?

I-- I'D LIKE THAT...

...VERY MUCH.

I'd been asked to hold myself in reserve until the first wave had landed.

Good for the men's morale, Deren said.

I could understand that.

Especially in the case of one particular man.

ENNIS!

WHUMP

OH!

UH... WE SHOULD GET BACK TO... THIS.

AH... YES...TAKING CONTROL OF THE SHIP...

"...AND MARKING IT WITH OUR SIGN.

"YOUR SIGN, SEPHIE."

I NEED TO SPEAK WITH YOUR LEADER!

CAN YOU DIRECT ME TO THE MINISTER OF MERIDIAN?

YOU'RE LOOKING FOR *ME*?

HE'S DONE IT.

HE'S REALLY GOING TO LET AN ISLAND FALL.

I--

MAYBE I CAN...

CRENNER!

I'M GOING AHEAD TO TORBEL!

MAYBE I CAN RENEW THE ORE THEY HAVE!

TELL EVERYONE!

"...THEN THEY'LL NEED ALL THE HELP THEY CAN GET TO EVACUATE THE ISLAND."

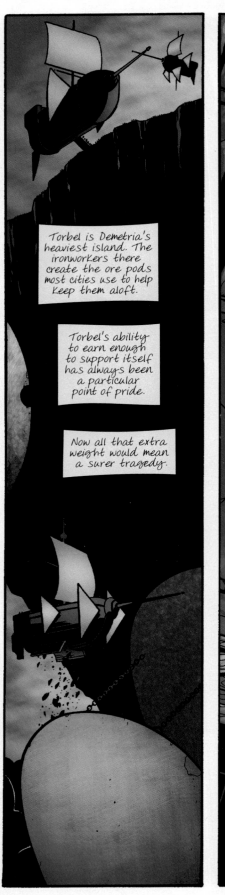

Torbel is Demetria's heaviest island. The ironworkers there create the ore pods most cities use to help keep them aloft.

Torbel's ability to earn enough to support itself has always been a particular point of pride.

Now all that extra weight would mean a surer tragedy.

Poor Torbel...imagine being able to hear, to feel, to sense that the ground beneath your feet was shearing away as its own shifting bulk began to break the island apart.

In the earliest days, some islands did fall.

But that was before we tamed them.

MINISTER RUDEF?

WE'RE GOING TO LOSE HUNDREDS OF PEOPLE...

...ALL OVER THE PRICE OF OUR PODS.

NO! IT'S NOT BEST IF YOU LOSE SO MANY!

HEAR ME, CHILD.

WHA--?

PUSH.

WHO--?

MINISTER RUDEF--

THIS TRAGEDY IS *NOT* OF *YOUR* MAKING, RUDY.

NO ONE COULD HAVE FORESEEN ILAHN'S MADNESS.

TORBEL WILL SURVIVE--HER PEOPLE ARE AS TENACIOUS AND DETERMINED AS THE IRON WE WORK.

NO--THOSE NOT KILLED WILL BE SCATTERED AMONG THE OTHER ISLANDS!

TORBEL IS *DEAD*, TRUPERT.

DEAD.

ALL BECAUSE OF THAT POWER-HUNGRY MADMAN--

...SWIFT WINDS ARE OURS!

GOOD GIRL.

WE'RE NOT MOVING FAST ENOUGH, BUT IF I *PUSH* OUR SHIPS...

EVERY ONE LEFT BEHIND, I'VE *KILLED.*

THEY WERE THE ATLANTEANS,

a peaceful civilization of artists and philosophers who used their phenomenal mental and physical skills to build an island utopia. They had but one responsibility: to guide and shepherd Earth's newborn race of *homo sapiens* towards a grand and glorious destiny. But when a mysterious cataclysm plunged Atlantis and its people beneath the waves, six — and only six — were awakened by a mysterious stranger one thousand centuries later to find their utopia forgotten and in ruins, their brothers and sisters caught in an unshakeable slumber. Capricia, their leader, has orchestrated a plan to revive Atlantis, but she'll have to enact it without Verityn's help, as he and the stranger are off having a very interesting conversation....

The mental and physical abilities of the Atlanteans are identical in nature but not in application. Capricia and her teammates have each channeled their abilities into different skills:

CAPRICIA	TUG	ZEPHYRE	GALVAN & GAMMID	VERITYN
Shapeshifter and empath	Telekinetic strongman	Hypermetabolic intellectual	Manipulators of the electromagnetic spectrum	Seer of all truths

Mark **WAID** WRITER   Steve **EPTING** PENCILER   Rick **MAGYAR** INKER   Frank **D'ARMATA** COLORIST   Dave **LANPHEAR** LETTERER

THE SHORT EXPLANATION IS **THIS:**

GRAVITY IS **OVERRATED.**

IT TAKES THE GRAVITATIONAL FORCE OF OUR **ENTIRE PLANET** TO HOLD A SHARD OF METAL **DOWN**--

--BUT EVEN THE **TINIEST MAGNET** CAN PICK IT **UP.**

ELECTROMAGNETIC FORCE IS THE **TRUE** POWERHOUSE. BECAUSE **MATTER**-- A.K.A. **FERMIONS**--AND **ENERGY**-- A.K.A. **BOSONS**-- ARE THE TWO **HALVES** OF ELECTROMAGNETISM--

--THEY AFFECT ONE ANOTHER SO **DIRECTLY** AND **DRAMATICALLY** THAT THE BEST **GRAVITY** CAN DO IS WATCH FROM THE **SIDELINES.**

ATLANTIS, LIKE **ALL** SOLID MATTER, IS ESSENTIALLY A COLLECTION OF **FERMIONS.**

AND SINCE THE TWINS **GALVAN** AND **GAMMID** ARE, FOR ALL INTENTS AND PURPOSES, **LIVING BOSONS**--

--**THEY** CAN WRENCH ATLANTIS **FREE** FROM THE CONSTRAINTS OF **EARTHLY GRAVITY.**

"...ACCOMPLISHING *SOMETHING!*"

--SHE'D BE *DEAD.*

WE ARE.

CAPRICIA!

I DON'T NEED TO HEAR ZEPHYRE SCREAMING. HER CRY COMES TELEPATHICALLY--

--AND WE'LL BE AT HER SIDE BEFORE THE SOUND OF HER VOICE COULD HAVE REACHED US.

JUST FROM HER TONE, I CAN TELL THIS ATTACK MAKES THE LAST ONE LOOK LIKE A PRACTICE RUN. I DID THE RIGHT THING IN DISMISSING VERITYN.

"--WE DON'T *HAVE* TO USE NULL-GRAV ON AN ENTIRE *ISLAND CITY*--

"--JUST ON THE VERMIN CRAWLING *THROUGH* IT!"

THEY'RE *GONE!*

THEN *DON'T STOP!* GIVE IT *EVERYTHING!* WE CAN *DO THIS!*

OUR *FRIENDS*-- OUR *FAMILIES*-- THEY'RE *COUNTING* ON US!

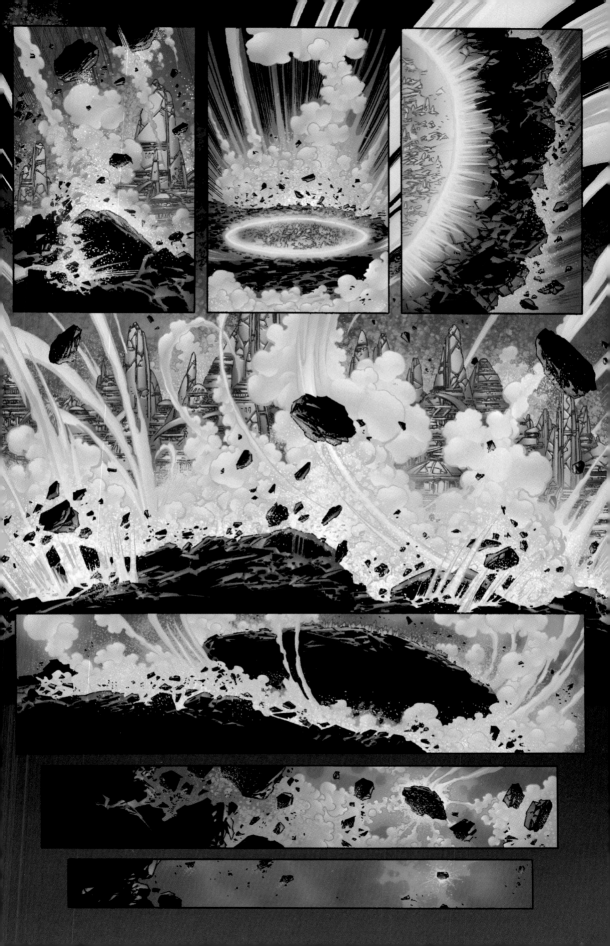

EVERYTHING'S **BLACK**.

I DON'T EVEN REALIZE MY EYES ARE **CLOSED** UNTIL I'M OVERCOME BY A **FAMILIAR SMELL**.

CHAPTER 5

VERITYN, WAKE *UP.* TODAY'S THE *BIG DAY.*

YOU MEAN WE'RE GOING WITH *DAD?*

YOUR FATHER ISN'T *JOINING* US...

...RIGHT... *NOW,* I MEAN.

Oh.

WE HAVE TO GET TO THE *STASIS CHAMBERS* BEFORE *TRANSITION.* YOU'LL BE *SAFE* THERE.

BUT *DAD--*

VERITYN, *PLEASE!* THIS IS *NOT* A DEBATE, AND WE HAVE *NO* TIME TO *WASTE!* GET *DRESSED...*

...SO I CAN CONTINUE USING YOU AS AN *EXCUSE*...AND PRAY THE GODS CAN *FORGIVE* ME FOR SUCH A VILE ACT.

I'M *NOT* FEARFUL FOR MY SON. I'M AFRAID OF ABANDONING A WORLD IN WHICH I FEEL *NEEDED.* WHERE MY ACHIEVEMENTS *MEAN* SOMETHING.

WHERE THEY *DEFINE* ME.

I'M AFRAID FOR *ME*...AND THAT IS WHAT *DAMNS* ME. IN GARWIN'S EYES, I AM LOVED BECAUSE I AM *STRONG.* TO ADMIT *FEAR*...

I CAN ONLY *IMAGINE* HIS *REVULSION.* I COULD NEVER *BEAR* HIS *DISGUST.*

I LOVE HIM TOO MUCH.

Next month in FORGE

Crux Chapters 6 - 8
Frustrated by countless setbacks, Capricia goes on a rampage.

The Path Chapter 1
Obo-san prepares to embark on his quest for vengeance,
but the emperor has other plans.

Meridian Chapters 19 & 20
With Torbel perilously threatened, Sephie vows vengeance on her Uncle Ilahn.

Negation Chapter 3
Stranded in space, Kaine's band of escapees struggle for their lives!

Sojourn Chapters 4 and 5
The mysterious cloaked woman entrusts Arwyn with a rare artifact.

Saurians Unnatural Selection Part 1
From the world of SIGIL, a mini-series that reminds us you are
what you eat!

CROSSGEN COMICS

Graphic Novels

THE FIRST 1
    Two Houses Divided $19.95   1-931484-04-X

THE FIRST 2
    Magnificent Tension $19.95   1-931484-17-1

MYSTIC 1
    Rite of Passage $19.95   1-931484-00-7

MYSTIC 2
    The Demon Queen $19.95   1-931484-06-6

MERIDIAN 1
    Flying Solo $19.95   1-931484-03-1

MERIDIAN 2
    Going to Ground $19.95   1-931484-09-0

SCION 1
    Conflict of Conscience $19.95   1-931484-02-3

SCION 2
    Blood for Blood $19.95   1-931484-08-2

SIGIL 1
    Mark of Power $19.95   1-931484-01-5

SIGIL 2
    The Marked Man $19.95   1-931484-07-4

CRUX 1
    Atlantis Rising $15.95   1-931484-14-7

SOJOURN 1
    From the Ashes $19.95   1-931484-15-5

CROSSGEN ILLUSTRATED
    Volume 1 $24.95   1-931484-05-8